Dear Parents:

Congratulations! Your child is taking the first steps on an exciting journey. The destination? Independent reading!

STEP INTO READING® will help your child get there. The program offers five steps to reading success. Each step includes fun stories and colorful art or photographs. In addition to original fiction and books with favorite characters, there are Step into Reading Non-Fiction Readers, Phonics Readers and Boxed Sets, Sticker Readers, and Comic Readers—a complete literacy program with something to interest every child.

Learning to Read, Step by Step!

Ready to Read Preschool–Kindergarten
• big type and easy words • rhyme and rhythm • picture clues
For children who know the alphabet and are eager to begin reading.

Reading with Help Preschool–Grade 1
• basic vocabulary • short sentences • simple stories
For children who recognize familiar words and sound out new words with help.

Reading on Your Own Grades 1–3
• engaging characters • easy-to-follow plots • popular topics
For children who are ready to read on their own.

Reading Paragraphs Grades 2–3
• challenging vocabulary • short paragraphs • exciting stories
For newly independent readers who read simple sentences with confidence.

Ready for Chapters Grades 2–4
• chapters • longer paragraphs • full-color art
For children who want to take the plunge into chapter books but still like colorful pictures.

STEP INTO READING® is designed to give every child a successful reading experience. The grade levels are only guides; children will progress through the steps at their own speed, developir

Remember, a lifetime love of reading starts wit

For Mom and Dad

CUPHEAD © and ™ 2023 StudioMDHR Entertainment Inc. THE CUPHEAD SHOW!™ based on the video game from StudioMDHR. Netflix™: Netflix, Inc. Used with permission.

All rights reserved. Published in the United States by Random House Children's Books, a division of Penguin Random House LLC, 1745 Broadway, New York, NY 10019, and in Canada by Penguin Random House Canada Limited, Toronto.

Step into Reading, Random House, and the Random House colophon are registered trademarks of Penguin Random House LLC.

Visit us on the Web!
StepIntoReading.com
rhcbooks.com

Educators and librarians, for a variety of teaching tools, visit us at RHTeachersLibrarians.com

ISBN 978-0-593-56578-0 (trade) — ISBN 978-0-593-56579-7 (lib. bdg.)
ISBN 978-0-593-56580-3 (ebook)

Printed in the United States of America

10 9 8 7 6 5 4 3 2 1

NETFLIX

THE CUPHEAD SHOW!

THE GREAT ESCAPE!

by Skye Yan

Random House 🏠 New York

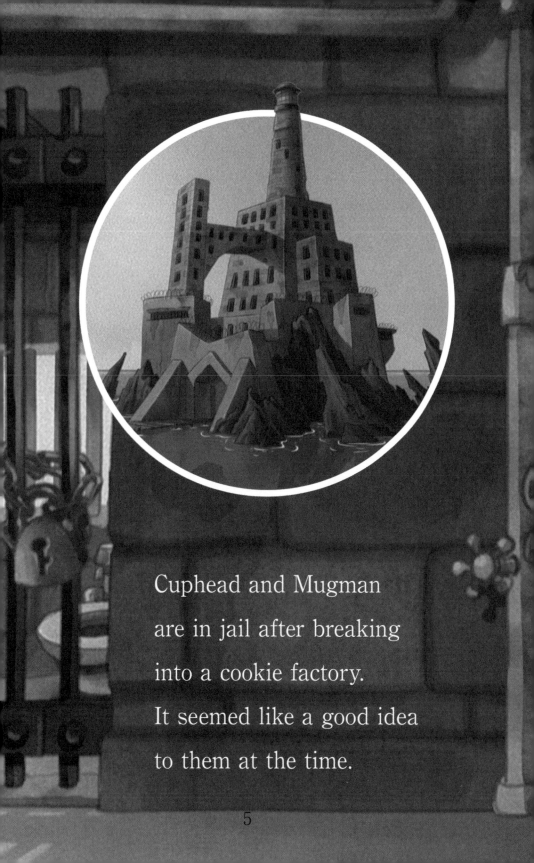

Cuphead and Mugman
are in jail after breaking
into a cookie factory.
It seemed like a good idea
to them at the time.

Jail is a scary place.
The other prisoners
are big and tough.
Miss Cyclops is the
biggest and toughest
of them all.

Mugman does not like

being in jail.

"Do not worry," Cuphead says.

He has an escape plan . . .

. . . but they do not get far
before they are chased
by guard dogs.

For punishment,
Cuphead and Mugman
have to break rocks.

Afterward, they try crawling
through the vents . . .

. . . but get caught again.

For punishment, they
get put into the Box.

They try digging
their way out . . .

. . . but get caught *again*.

For punishment,
they get put in the Box
and have to break rocks!

THE BOX

Mugman wants to give up.
He thinks the only way out
is by doing their time.

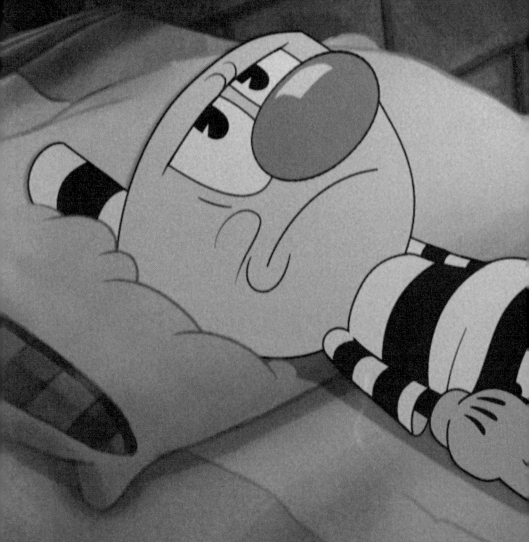

But Cuphead keeps trying.

He comes up with a new plan.

Mugman makes the best
of his time in jail.
He works at the machines . . .

. . . and plays jacks

with the other prisoners.

He patches their socks

and does their laundry.

Meanwhile,
Cuphead steals
a spoon from the dining hall.
Mugman makes Miss Cyclops
a pink blanket that is nice and soft,
just the way she likes it.

Cuphead is ready to break out,
but Mugman wants to stay.
The brothers say goodbye.

Cuphead digs a tunnel
with the spoon he took
from the dining hall.

But his plan does not work!

He ends up right where he started.

Cuphead finally gives up.

Mugman is worried.

Cuphead never gives up.

Mugman cannot stand to see

his brother like this.

"Okay, let us go," he says.

They will break out together!

Mugman hides Cuphead

in a cart.

They are going to escape

in the laundry truck!

Miss Cyclops shows up.

She does not want Mugman to go.

Who will wash her blanket?

Mugman tells her not to worry.

His place is with Cuphead.

Miss Cyclops understands.

Miss Cyclops takes off her ball
and chain and puts it around the boys.
Then she swings them around
and around, and throws Cuphead
and Mugman over the wall . . .

. . . and all the way home.

FREEDOM!

The brothers have never been
so happy to see their cottage.

Elder Kettle greets the brothers
at the door—and then grounds
them for life.
That sounds great to them!